The Nursery Collection

Miss Bilberry's
New House

Emma Chichester Clark

$\mathcal{M}$iss Bilberry lived in a pale yellow house with a fine view of the mountains. She had a dog whose name was Cecilie, a cat called Chester, and two birds called Chitty and Chatty.

Every day, Miss Bilberry jumped out of bed, brushed her teeth, dressed, put on her hat and had breakfast in the shade of the broad-leaved tree, looking out at the blue mountains.

After breakfast she swept the path with a thin reed broom and fed the birds and animals. She watered the flowers and vegetables growing in her garden and had a light lunch on the verandah.

Then she had a nap in her hammock between two swaying palms,
and supper under the stars. Sometimes she played her violin
and sang a few songs, and then she went to bed.

It was a lovely life, and if it weren't for
one thing, Miss Bilberry would have
been completely happy…

She just couldn't stop wondering whether
she might not be even happier if she lived on
the other side of the mountains. The more she looked,
the more she wondered.

One day, Miss Bilberry jumped out of bed and said,
"Everybody up! Today's the day for moving house!
Let's start packing!"
They filled all their boxes, baskets and bags and put
everything on to a wobbly old cart.

They waved goodbye to the house and the garden, the
broad-leaved tree and the two swaying palms, and set
off towards the blue mountains.
"Oh, I'm so excited," cried Miss Bilberry, "I just can't wait
to get to the other side!"

They walked and pushed the cart for many miles, through fields

and forests,

through rain

and sunshine,

uphill,

and downhill.

In some places the flowers were taller than Miss Bilberry!
They could hardly see where they were going.
"This is the wrong way," snarled Chester.
"No it isn't," snapped Cecilie.
They argued for hours. It nearly drove Miss Bilberry mad.

Miss Bilberry climbed a tree, but she still wasn't sure where they
were. Should they go left or right? She had no idea at all.
"Do stop quarrelling, you two," she said, "everything is going to
be fine when we get to the other side."

On and on they went, through days and nights. The further they
went, the more lost they became, and it felt as though the journey
would never end.

"I want to go back to our lovely old house," said Cecilie.
"I want to go home," moaned Chester.
"If you don't stop grumbling I'll leave you right here!"
said Miss Bilberry.

Miss Bilberry sent Chitty and Chatty ahead. They could fly
above the trees and see where to go next, but they weren't very
clever, so they usually forgot where they'd been.

"They're *hopeless*!" snarled Chester. "We could sit here for days
before they find us again. I expect we're going round in circles."
But one day, Chitty and Chatty returned, their shrieks
echoing all over the forest.
"We're there! We're there! Come and see!
A lovely house! Come and see."

And there it was...
"Oh my!" gasped Miss Bilberry. "Oh my, oh my!
It's perfection. It's just as I thought it would be!"

"Thank goodness for that," sighed Chester. It wasn't very far to go, just a few fields, down a hill and through a meadow.

They ran all the way.   They unloaded the cart and
emptied the bags. Chester sniffed the air and looked puzzled.
"It's strange," he thought, "but I feel as if I've been here before."

Miss Bilberry was so tired that she slept all afternoon in the hammock that she strung between two swaying palms, exactly like before. Then she made a stew from the vegetables growing in the garden and they all began to feel better.

Each morning the sun shone. Miss Bilberry smiled as she leapt out of bed, and her life seemed better than ever. Her breakfast was more delicious, the mountains more beautiful, the animals more cheerful. They were all happier than ever before.

Only Chester gave Miss Bilberry a funny look now and
then, but she never knew what he was thinking. Sometimes she
lay awake and remembered their long journey, it must have been
about a hundred miles. She was pleased with the way things had
turned out, even though some quite peculiar things had
happened lately...

The first was that Miss Bilberry had found her very own old
tooth-brush in the bathroom. Then she found Cecilie's bowl
in the garden, and a very old sock she'd been knitting before they
moved was under her bed. How did they get there?
Miss Bilberry gazed out at the mountains and wondered.
Do you know what she was wondering?

Chester, the clever cat, watched her and smiled to himself.
You have probably guessed by now that Miss Bilberry's new
house was not a new house at all, but Miss Bilberry... well, if she
did know, she didn't say a word to anybody, and they all lived
there happily ever after.

The end

2

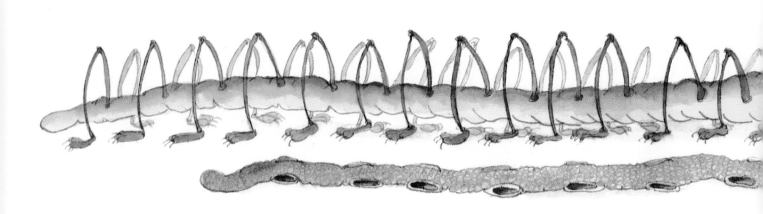

The Trouble
with Gran

Babette Cole

The trouble with Gran is . . .

. . . secretly . . .

she's an alien!

None of the other OAPs suspected a thing . . .

. . . until our teacher tried to organise an outing for them, to Wethorp, as our school project!

"But we want to go somewhere hot and exciting!" said Gran.
"Sit down and be quiet!" snapped teacher.

Wethorp was awful.

Gran started to play up!

We went to an Old Time Music Hall.

Gran did not like the singing!

And there was a Glamorous Grandma Contest.

. . . Gran cheated of course!

She really livened up the fun fair!

We were asked to leave the amusement arcade!

On the Lunar Landscape Tour
Gran met some friends.

She took them to the tea rooms!

So we missed the bus home.
Teacher blamed Gran!

"We've had enough of this dump!" said Gran.
"Fasten safety-belts!"

We zoomed towards Gran's planet . . .

and landed just in time for carnival!

Gran did the Limbo . . .

. . . and climbed a bloomernut tree.

We were sad to leave, but Gran had to get home to feed the cat.

We landed in the school playground
with a bump!

Mum and Dad marched Gran away.
"You're too old for that sort of thing now,"
they said.
"That's what they think," muttered Gran.

And when she got home she opened her own travel agency . . .

. . . in Dad's garage!

PLUM TREE COTTAGE

A Doll's House Story

written and illustrated by
Elaine Mills

Once upon a time there was a little wooden doll called Peggy.

And she lived by herself in the forest because she had *no* home.

One day there was an icy wind. It blew and blew
until all the trees were bare.
It was time for Peggy to look for a place of her own.
So she packed up her bag and off she went.

She walked along the road until she came to a house.

Knock! Knock! Knock!

She banged on the door.

"Hello!" said a man. "Who are you?
And what do you want?"

"I am Peggy Doll," she told him.

"And I have *no* home. Have you
got room for me?"

"Well," said the man, "you can see for yourself..."

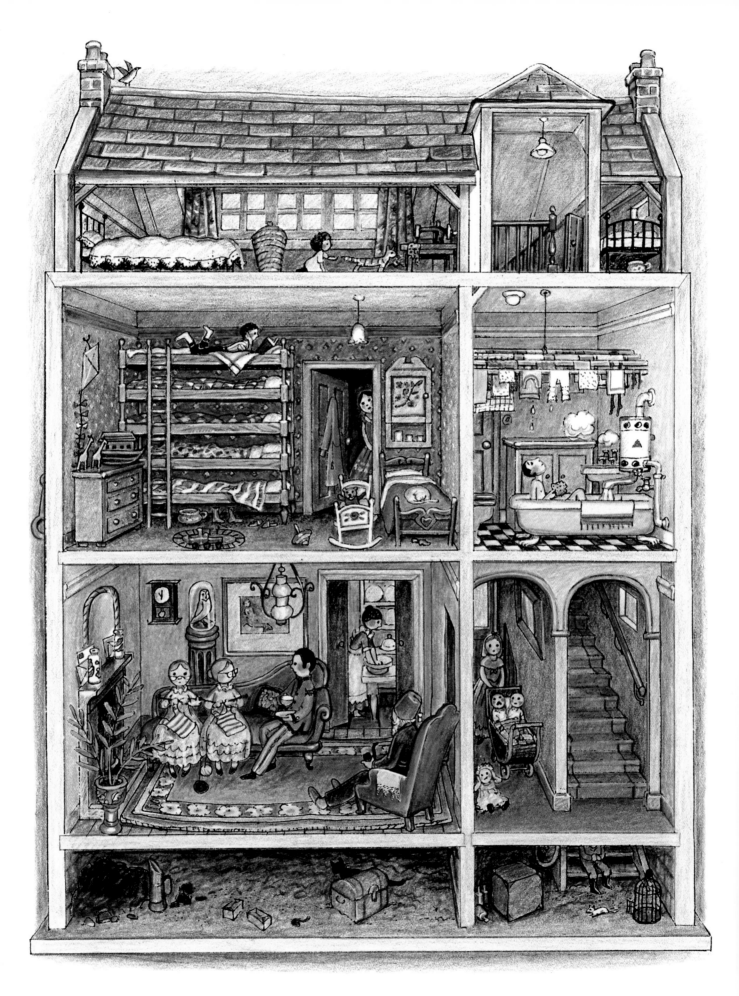

"…there are too many of us in here already."

"But where can I go?" asked Peggy.

"Try at the manor," he told her.

"There's plenty of room at the manor."

"Thank you," said Peggy.

She walked along the road until she came to the manor.
It was a large blue house with a row of windows in the roof.

Ding-a-ling-a-ling! Peggy rang the bell.
A lady in a long velvet gown came to open the door.
"Who are you?" she demanded. "What do you want?"
"My name is Peggy Doll," said Peggy.
"And I have *no* home. Have you got room for me?"

"Certainly not!" said the lady. "You have mud on your boots!"
"But where can I go?" asked Peggy.
"There's an empty cottage further up the lane,"
the lady told her. "Go away!"

Peggy trudged along the lane. She felt cold and sad.

The rain was running down her neck and her dress was wet.

At last she came to a house.

It was Plum Tree Cottage.
She knocked on the door. But nobody came.

She shouted through the letterbox. There was no reply.
So Peggy opened the door and stepped inside.

First she explored upstairs.

And then she explored downstairs.

Plum Tree Cottage was just right.
So she lit a fire in the living room and sat down to enjoy it.

But what was that? *Rat-a-tat-tat!*
Somebody tapping on the door!

It was Rabbit.

"Can I come in?" said Rabbit. "Please? My burrow
is full of water and I don't know where to go!"

"Of course you can," said Peggy.

Peggy took off his wet coat and hung it up to dry.
"Let's have tea by the fire," she said.
"And I shall tell you a story."

Rabbit snuggled up beside her on the chair
and looked at all the pictures.
"I like it here," said Rabbit. "Can I stay?"

So Peggy Doll gave Rabbit a bedroom in the attic.

And they both lived happily ever after,
in their own little cottage
at the end of the lane.

4

Row Your Boat

rhyme by
Pippa Goodhart

illustrations by
Stephen Lambert

Hoist, hoist, hoist the sail
We're setting out to sea.
We're sailing to an island,
Georgie, you and me.

Leap, leap, leap ashore,
Jump onto the land.
Splashing in the water,
And kicking up the sand.

Thump, bump, humpety-bump,
Who's that on the track?
A great big friendly elephant!
Let's climb up on his back.

Flap, flap, fluttering wings,
Birds fly all around.
Hold on to the elephant's ears,
We're far above the ground.

Slip, slip, slip and slide,
Down the elephant's nose,
To see the snakes and spiders
That live down by his toes.

Up, jump, hurry along,
Clambering through the plants.
I can see the monkeys!
Let's join them in their dance.

Swing from arms, swing from tails,
Swooping through the trees.
Shaking all the flowers down
And making Georgie sneeze.
Achoo!

Push, poke, tug and pull.
The monkeys like to tease.
They pull the tail of something big
That's hiding in the trees.

Grr, grr! What's that noise?
Oooh! It's a lion's roar!
Quick! He's chasing after us,
Let's race back to the shore.

Run, run! Find the boat
And push it out to sea.
Before the lion catches us
And eats us for his tea!

Row, row, row your boat
Gently down the stream.
Merrily, merrily, merrily, merrily,
Life is but a dream.

Hoist, hoist, hoist the sail
We're setting out to sea.
We're sailing to an island,
Georgie, you and me.

Leap, leap, leap ashore,
Jump onto the land.
Splashing in the water,
And kicking up the sand.

Thump, bump, humpety-bump,
Who's that on the track?
A great big friendly elephant!
Let's climb up on his back.

Flap, flap, fluttering wings,
Birds fly all around.
Hold on to the elephant's ears,
We're far above the ground.

Slip, slip, slip and slide,
Down the elephant's nose,
To see the snakes and spiders
That live down by his toes.

Up, jump, hurry along,
Clambering through the plants.
I can see the monkeys!
Let's join them in their dance.

Swing from arms, swing from tails,
Swooping through the trees,
Shaking all the flowers down
And making Georgie sneeze.
Achoo!

Push, poke, tug and pull.
The monkeys like to tease.
They pull the tail of something big
That's hiding in the trees.

Grr, grr! What's that noise?
Oooh! It's a lion's roar!
Quick! He's chasing after us,
Let's race back to the shore.

Run, run! Find the boat
And push it out to sea.
Before the lion catches us
And eats us for his tea!

Row, row, row your boat
Gently up the stream.
Merrily, merrily, merrily, merrily,
Was it just a dream?

5

Cat's Colours

Jane Cabrera

Yellow

Purple

Blue

Orange

Red

White

Brown

Green

Pink

Black

Is it Green?
Green is the grass
where I like to walk.

Is it
Pink?
Pink are the petals
of my favourite
flowers.

Is it
Black?
Black is the night
when bats
swoop and soar.

Is it **Red?**
Red is the rug
where I snooze
by the fire.

Is it *Yellow*?

Yellow is the sand on the sunny beach.

Is it Brown?
Brown is the earth
where I dig my holes.

Is it White?

White are the clouds floating in the sky.

Is it Orange?

Yes! Because...

Orange is the colour of Mummy.

6

One Smiling Grandma

A CARIBBEAN COUNTING BOOK

ANNE MARIE LINDEN

Illustrated by
LYNNE RUSSELL

1

One smiling grandma in a rocking chair,

2

Two yellow bows tied on braided hair.

3

Three hummingbirds sipping nectar sweet,

4

Four steel drums tapping out the beat.

5

Five flying fish gliding through the air,

6

Six market ladies selling their wares.

7

Seven conch shells I find on the beach,

8

Eight sugar apples, just out of reach.

9

Nine hairy coconuts, hard and round,

10

Ten sleepy mongoose,

Hush!

Not a sound.

7

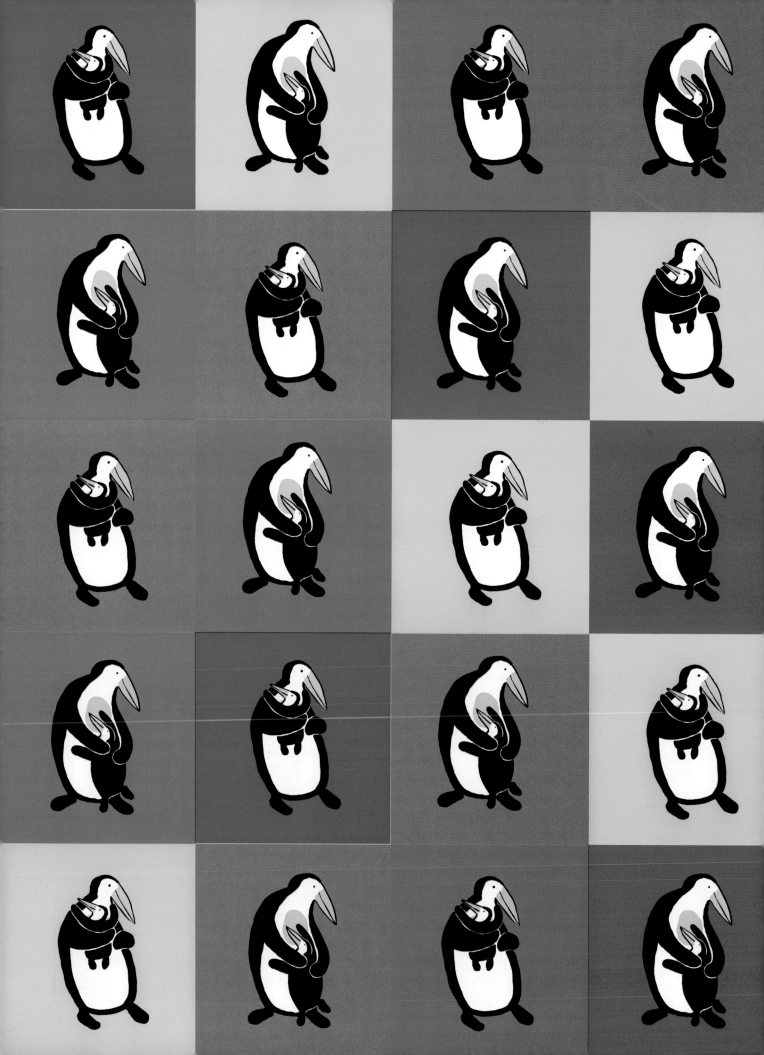

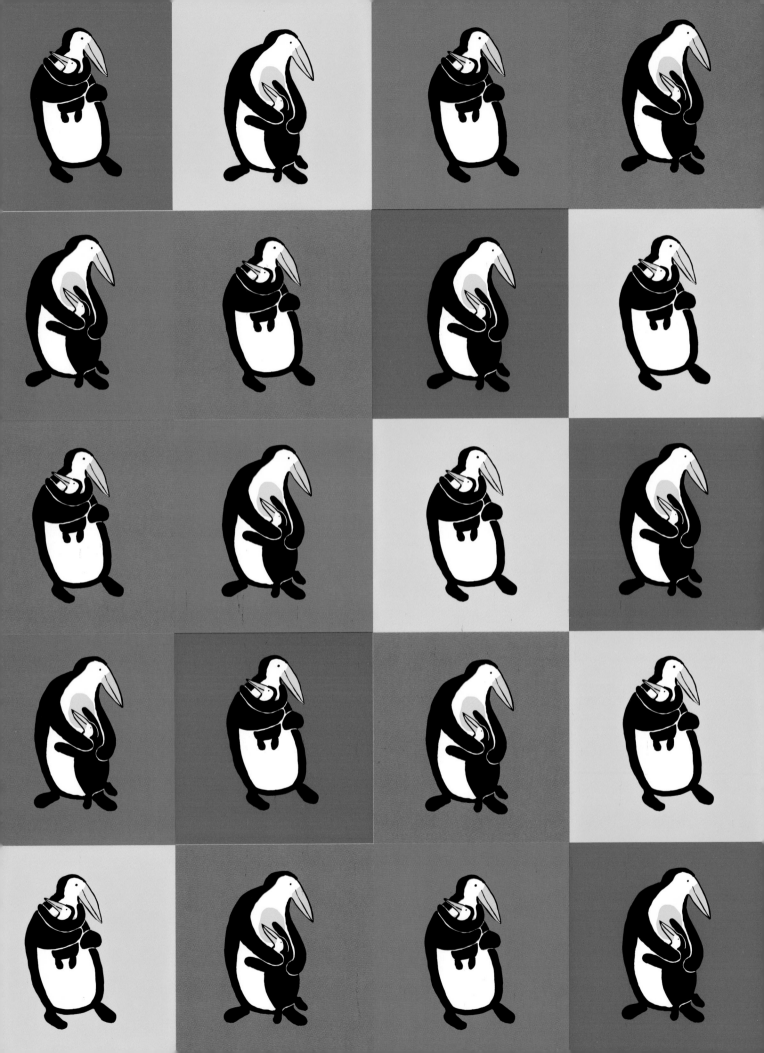

I like it when.....

Mary Murphy

I like it
when
you
hold
my
hand

I like it
when
you
let
me
help

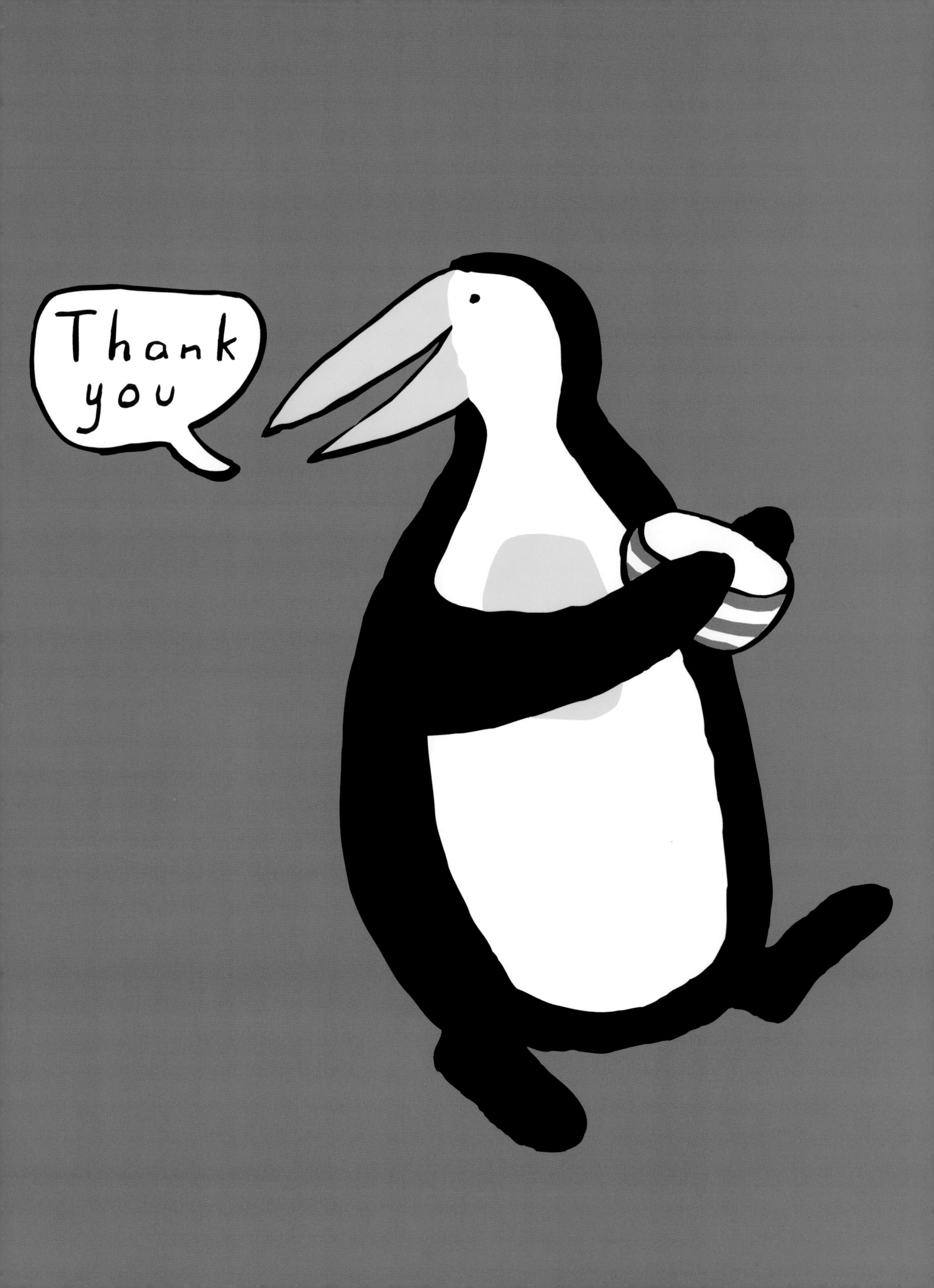
Thank you

I like it when we

I like it when we

play peekaboo

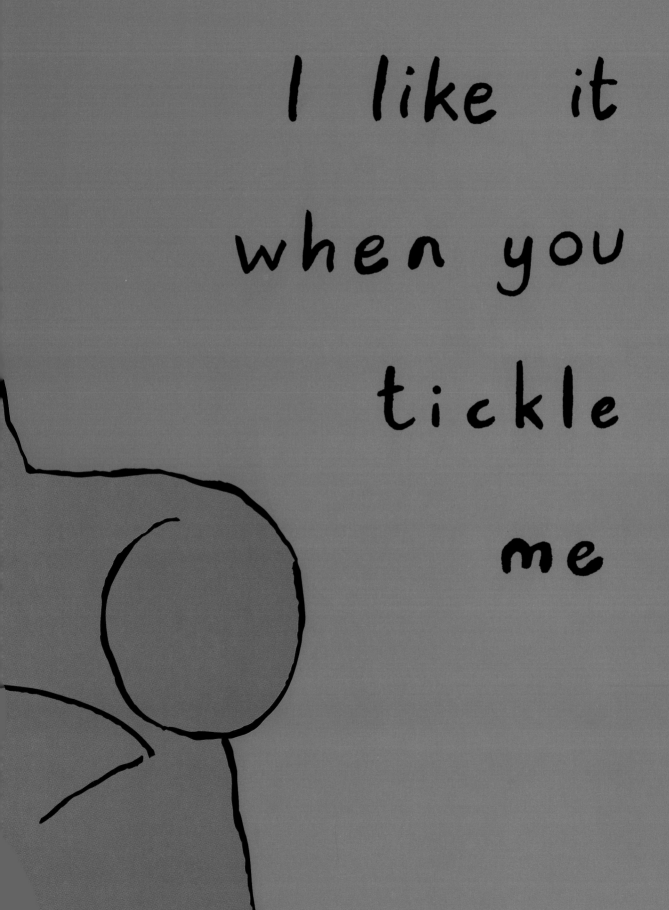

I like it when

you dance with me

I like it
when
you
read
me
stories

I like it when

you hug me tight

I like it when we
we splash about

I like it

when

we

kiss

goodnight

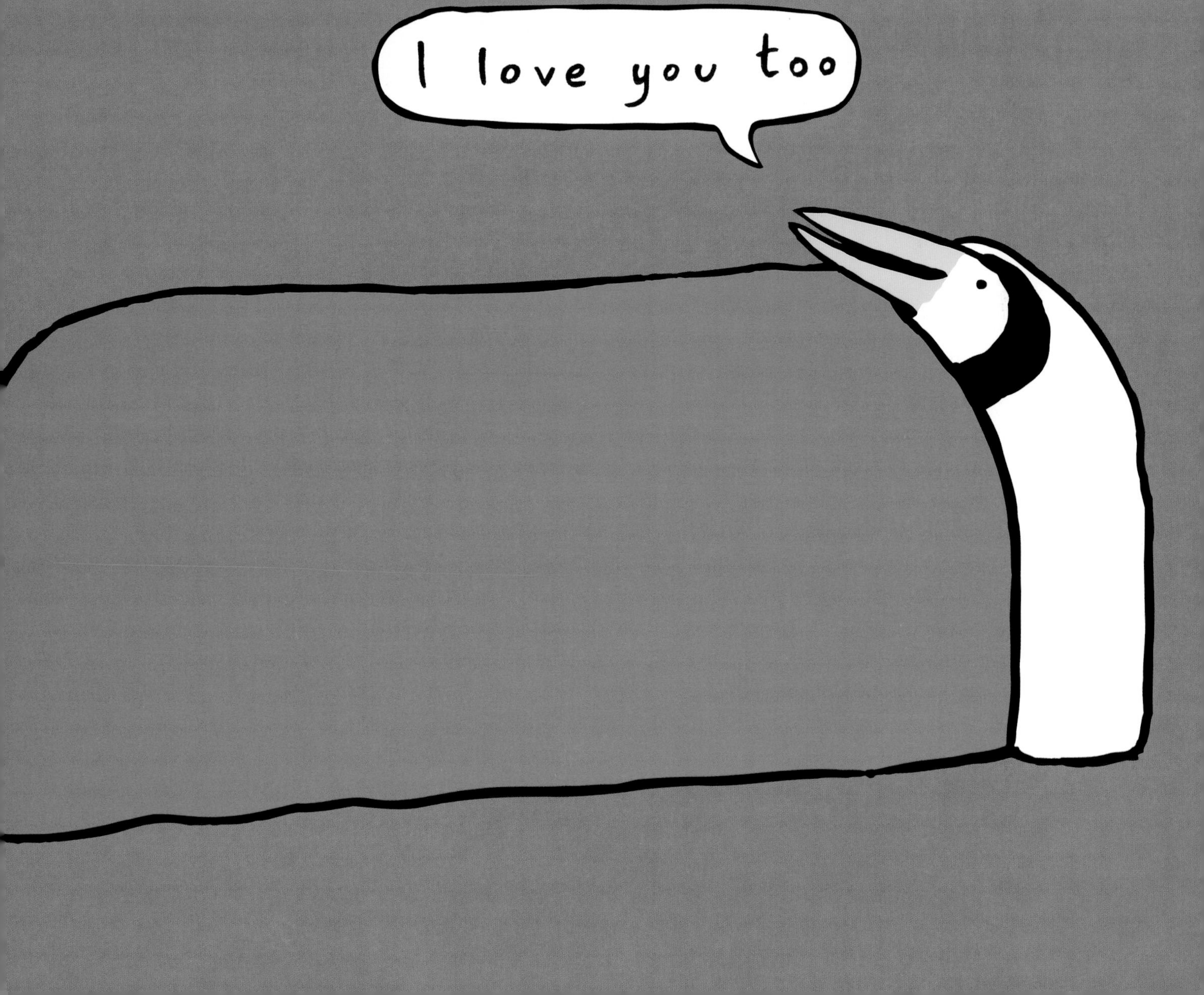
I love you too

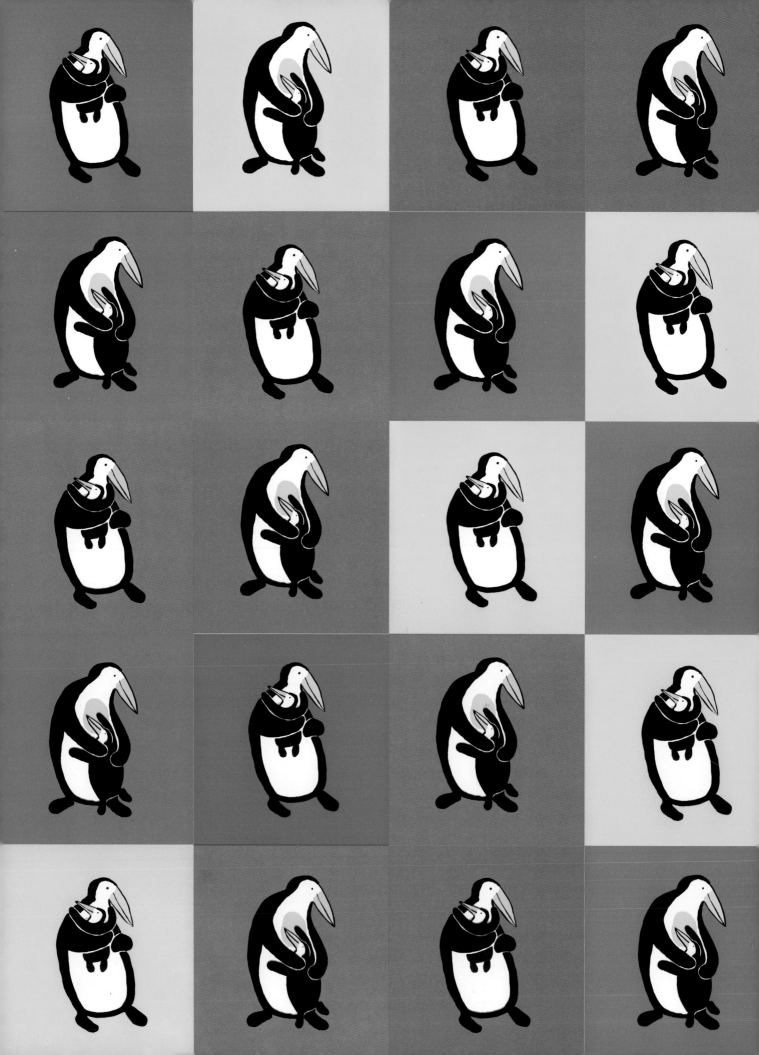

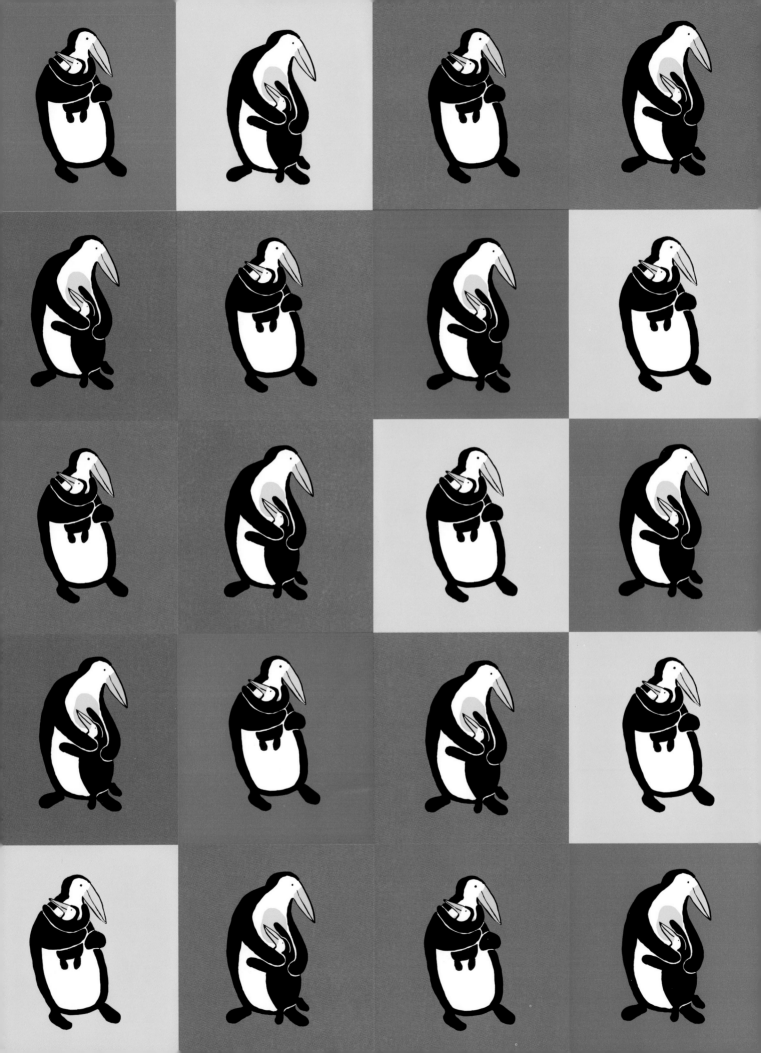

Julia Donaldson
A Squash and a Squeeze

Illustrated by Axel Scheffler

A little old lady lived all by herself
With a table and chairs and a jug on the shelf.

A wise old man heard her grumble and grouse,
"There's not enough room in my house.
Wise old man, won't you help me please?
My house is a squash and a squeeze."

"Take in your hen," said the wise old man.

"Take in my hen? What a curious plan."

Well, the hen laid an egg on the fireside rug,

And flapped round the room knocking over the jug.

The little old lady cried, "What shall I do?
It was poky for one and it's tiny for two.
My nose has a tickle and there's no room to sneeze.
My house is a squash and a squeeze."

And she said, "Wise old man, won't you help me please?
My house is a squash and a squeeze."

"Take in your goat," said the wise old man.

"Take in my goat? What a curious plan."

Well, the goat chewed the curtains and trod on the egg,

Then set down to nibbling the table leg.

The little old lady cried, "Glory me!
It was tiny for two and it's titchy for three.
The hen pecks the goat and the goat's got fleas.
My house is a squash and a squeeze."

And she said, "Wise old man, won't you help me please?
My house is a squash and a squeeze."

"Take in your pig," said the wise old man.

"Take in my pig? What a curious plan."

So she took in her pig who kept chasing the hen,

And raiding the larder again and again.

The little old lady cried, "Stop, I implore!
It was titchy for three and it's teeny for four.
Even the pig in the larder agrees,
My house is a squash and a squeeze."

And she said, "Wise old man, won't you help me please?
My house is a squash and a squeeze."

"Take in your cow," said the wise old man.

"Take in my cow? What a curious plan."

Well, the cow took one look and charged straight at the pig,
Then jumped on the table and tapped out a jig.

The little old lady cried, "Heavens alive!
It was teeny for four and it's weeny for five.
I'm tearing my hair out, I'm down on my knees.
My house is a squash and a squeeze."

And she said, "Wise old man, won't you help me please?
My house is a squash and a squeeze."

"Take them all out," said the wise old man.
"But then I'll be back where I first began."

So she opened the window and out flew the hen.
"That's better – at last I can sneeze again."

She shooed out the goat and she shoved out the pig.
"My house is beginning to feel pretty big."

She huffed and she puffed and she pushed out the cow.
"Just look at my house, it's enormous now.

Thank you, old man, for the work you have done.
It was weeny for five, it's gigantic for one.
There's no need to grumble and there's no need to grouse.
There's plenty of room in my house."

And now she's full of frolics and fiddle-de-dees.
It isn't a squash and it isn't a squeeze.

Yes she's full of frolics and fiddle-de-dees.
It isn't a squash or a squeeze.

9

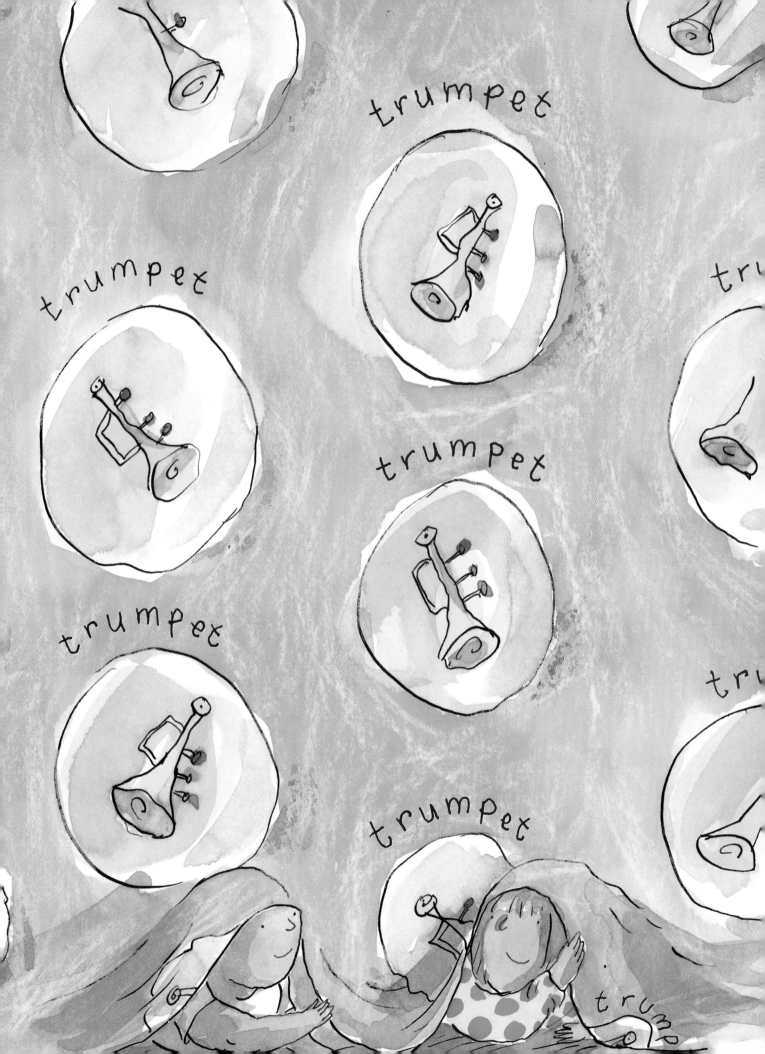

We're Not Tired

.Selina Young.

"Hello, I'm Ness and this is my brother, Hamish.
It's bedtime and we've put on our pyjamas.
Mum's come to tuck us in and turn out the light."

"I'm not tired," I say, when Mum's
gone downstairs.

"Let's play tents," says Hamish.
Teddy joins in too because he can't sleep either.

"Let's dress up," I say. "We could be explorers."

"But explorers quietly, so Mum won't hear."

"Hunting for buried treasure."

"Come on, let's build a rocket," I say.
"I'll be the captain and we'll fly to the moon,"
says Hamish.

"We might get captured by aliens."

"And have to fight them off."

"I'm fed up with aliens. G R R R R R.
I'm a tiger now," I say, in a very tigery way.

We go growling and prowling through the jungle.
"My tiger's knees are sore," I say.

"Let's be dancers," Hamish says.

So we ring and we rose right round the room.

We go huffing and puffing . . .

And dancing and prancing . . .

And trumpeting and tooting.

Then SUDDENLY…

…we hear footsteps on the stairs!

"Quick, get into bed!" I say.

Everything's quiet and Mum thinks
we're asleep. So she tiptoes away.

"It's all right, she's gone," says Hamish.
"Let's pretend to be mice who are creeping
and squeaking."
"My mouse is thinking of sleeping," I whisper.
"Mine too."
We snuggle down deep under the covers.

"I'm tired now," I say.

"Me too," whispers Hamish.
"Let's play sleeping."

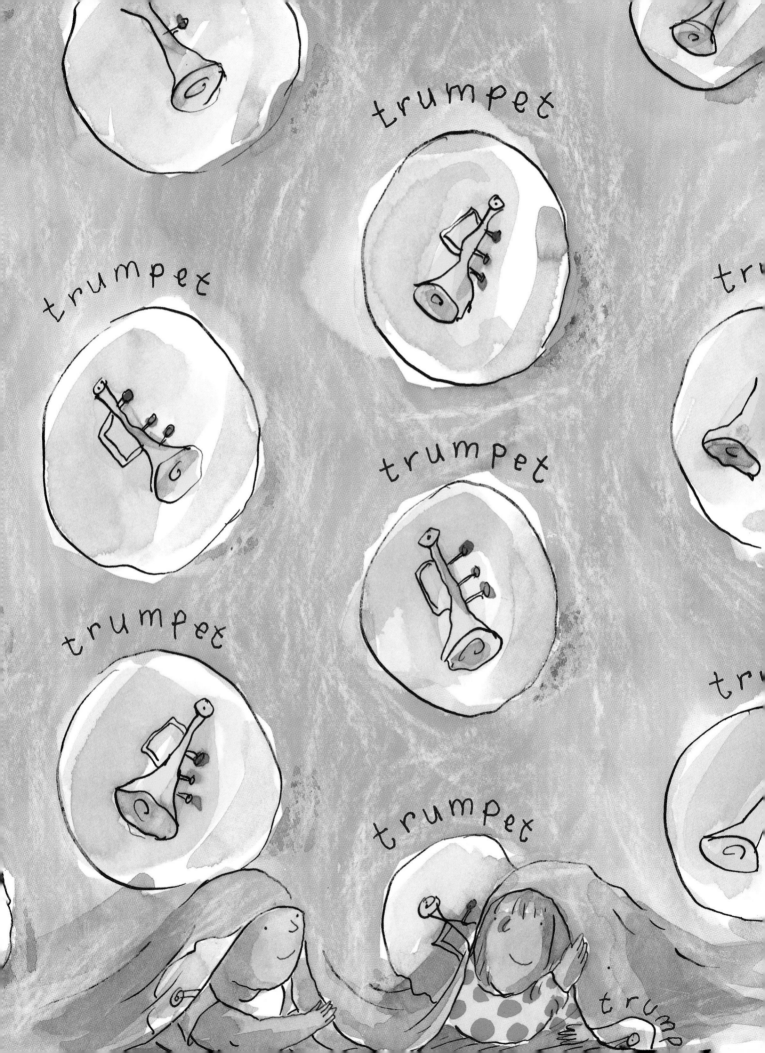

10

ELLA AND THE NAUGHTY LION

written by

ANNE COTTRINGER

pictures by

RUSSELL AYTO

The day Ella's mother
   came home with baby Jasper, a lion
   slipped in through the door.

He was a very naughty lion.

He pulled off Jasper's blanket.

He crept into Jasper's cot

and stretched out in a long yawn.
There was no room for Jasper.

When Ella's mother fed Jasper, the lion roared
so loudly, the whole house shook.

The lion tore up Jasper's soft brown teddy

and then chewed it into little wet bits.

"Naughty lion," said Ella. "That was Jasper's favourite teddy! Don't you ever do that again!"

But sometimes the lion was a good lion.
When Ella's grandmother took Ella out
for the day, the lion went too.
He wasn't a naughty lion at all.

He slid down the slide with Ella.

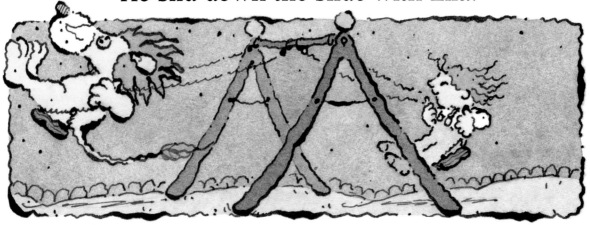

He swung on the swing.

He got dizzy from whizzing round the roundabout with Ella and her friends.

But when they got home, the lion
jumped into Jasper's bath . . .

and splashed water
all over the bathroom.

The next day, Jasper had
the snuffles and couldn't get to sleep.
He was very grizzly.

Ella wanted her mother to
play zoos with her.

"I can't, Ella. I'm too busy
with Jasper," said her mother.

"Why don't you go to the supermarket
with Daddy and maybe he'll buy
something nice to eat!"

But Ella didn't want anything nice to eat.
She was very unhappy. So was the lion,
and he was naughtier than ever!

He galloped up and down the aisles.

He knocked over stacks of baked beans

and crashed through a pyramid of oranges.

He gobbled up some cakes and got pink icing
all over his whiskers.

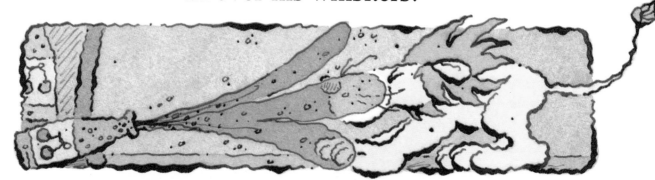

He spilled a big bottle of fizzy red cherryade
that spurted like a fountain over everything.

He roared so loudly that he frightened all
the people at the checkout.

"Bad, bad, bad lion!" Ella scolded him all the way home.
"Don't you ever behave like that again!"

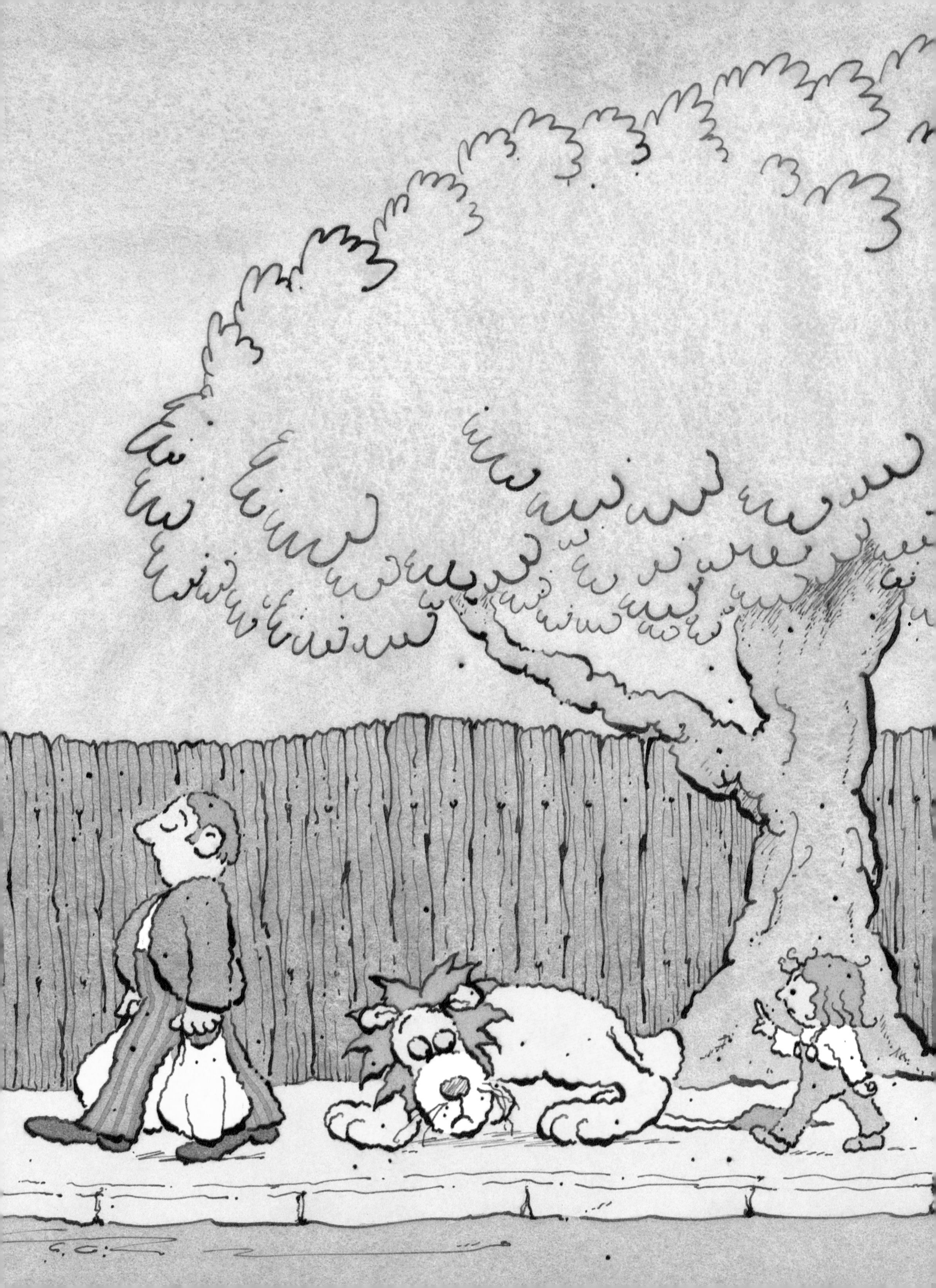

When they got home,
Jasper was asleep in his pram.
Ella's father squeezed past with
his shopping bags.

The naughty lion bounded in behind him and
bumped Jasper's pram.

It started
to roll

towards the
open door,

and before
anyone
knew it,

the pram was
bouncing down
the steps.

Ella and the lion watched with wide eyes.
Then the lion roared a big roar.

In a flash, Ella leaped
and caught hold of Jasper as
he sailed through the air.

Ella's mother and father rushed out.
"Oh Ella! What would we do
without you!" cried her mother.
"Well done," said her father.
The lion growled deep down
inside his throat.

Ella's mother
made some
hot chocolate.

Ella sat on the sofa
with Jasper gurgling
happily in her arms.
Ella smiled at her
baby brother and
gave his rattle
a little shake.

The lion got a
very grumpy look
on his face.
He flicked his
tail back and forth,
but Ella didn't notice.

And so the lion
slipped out just as
he had come in.

But from time to
time Ella heard a little
growl at the door.

The Nursery Collection
first published in Great Britain 1999
by Mammoth, an imprint of
Egmont Children's Books Limited
239 Kensington High Street, London W8 6SA

ISBN 0 7497 4055 8

10 9 8 7 6 5 4 3 2 1

A CIP catalogue record for this title is available from the British Library

Printed by Graficas Estella, Spain

Editor: Alison Ritchie
Designer: Jessica Meserve

This volume copyright © 1999 Egmont Children's Books Limited

Miss Bilberry's New House
by Emma Chichester Clark
First published in Great Britain 1993
by Methuen Children's Books Ltd, an
imprint of Egmont Children's Books Limited
Copyright © Emma Chichester Clark 1993

The Trouble With Gran
by Babette Cole
First published in Great Britain 1987
by William Heinemann Ltd, an imprint of
Egmont Children's Books Limited
Copyright © Babette Cole 1987
Babette Cole has asserted her moral rights

Plum Tree Cottage
by Elaine Mills
First published in Great Britain 1994
by Heinemann Young Books, an imprint of
Egmont Children's Books Limited
Copyright © Elaine Mills 1994

Row Your Boat
by Pippa Goodhart and Stephen Lambert
First published in Great Britain 1997
by William Heinemann Ltd, an imprint of
Egmont Children's Books Limited
Text copyright © Pippa Goodhart 1997
Illustrations copyright © Stephen Lambert 1997

Cat's Colours
by Jane Cabrera
First published in Great Britain 1997
by Heinemann Young Books and Mammoth,
imprints of Egmont Children's Books Limited
Copyright © Jane Cabrera 1997

One Smiling Grandma
by Anne Marie Linden and Lynne Russell
First published in Great Britain 1992
by William Heinemann Ltd, an imprint of
Egmont Children's Books Limited
Text copyright © Anne Marie Linden 1992
Illustrations © Lynne Russell 1992

I Like It When . . .
by Mary Murphy
First published in Great Britain 1997
by Methuen Children's Books Ltd and
Mammoth, imprints of
Egmont Children's Books Limited
Copyright © Mary Murphy 1997

A Squash and a Squeeze
by Julia Donaldson and Axel Scheffler
First published in Great Britain 1993
by Methuen Children's Books Ltd, an imprint
of Egmont Children's Books Limited
Text copyright © Julia Donaldson 1993
Illustrations copyright © Axel Scheffler 1993
Julia Donaldson and Axel Scheffler have
asserted their moral rights

We're Not Tired
by Selina Young
First published in Great Britain 1993
by William Heinemann Ltd, an imprint of
Egmont Children's Books Limited
Copyright © Selina Young 1993

Ella and the Naughty Lion
by Anne Cottringer and Russell Ayto
First published in Great Britain 1996
by William Heinemann Ltd, an imprint of
Egmont Children's Books Limited
Text copyright © Anne Cottringer 1996
Illustrations copyright © Russell Ayto 1996
The author and illustrator have asserted their
moral rights

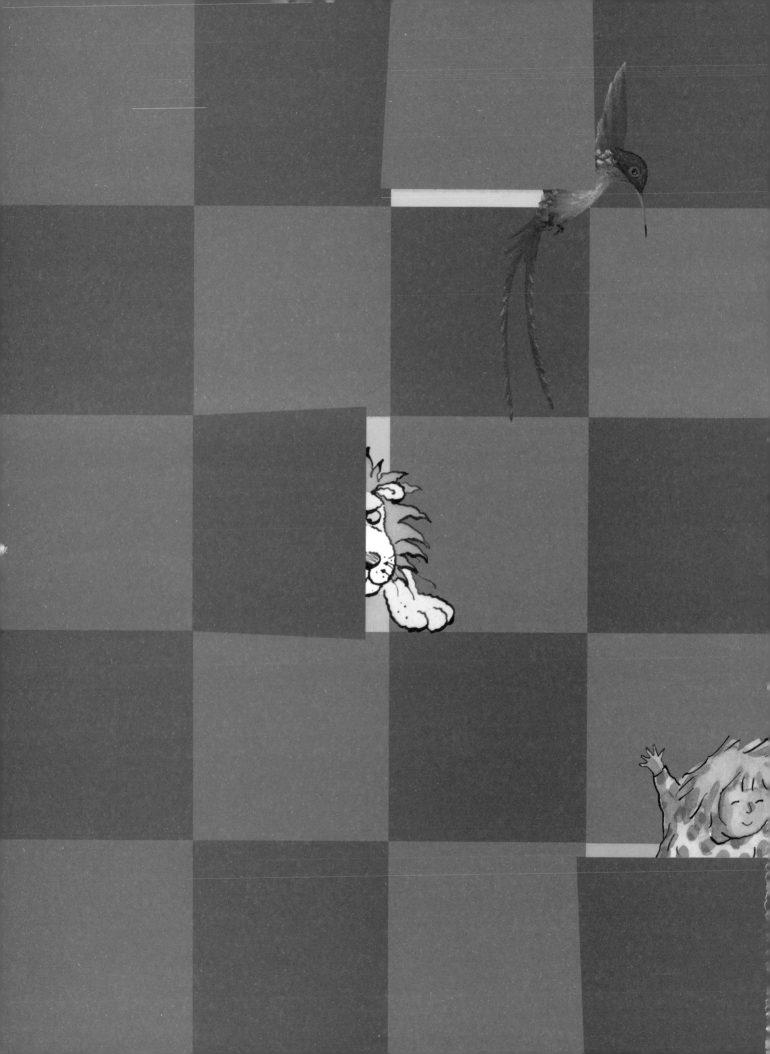